Prehistory of Fermanagh:

Stone-Age Hunters to Saints and Scholars

Helen Lanigan Wood

Fermanagh County Museum

Acknowledgements

I would like to thank the Northern Ireland Museums Council for its generous contribution towards the cost of this publication. I would also like to thank those who helped with research, Dr. Greer Ramsey of Armagh County Museum, Brian Williams of the Environment and Heritage Service, Sarah Gormley of Queen's University, Belfast, Richard Warner of the Ulster Museum and Tony Candon of the Ulster History Park.

I am very grateful to those who provided photographs, Patricia McLean, Ulster Museum and the Trustees of the Museums and Galleries of Northern Ireland, Niamh Deegan and the National Museum of Ireland, Mike Hartwell and Tony Corey of the Environment and Heritage Service, Alistair Carty of Archaeoptics Ltd, Dr. Ann Hamlin, and Richard Pierce. (Full credits inside back cover).

Finally, I would like to thank my colleague, Bronagh Cleary, for her helpful comments and for her work on the map.

Supported by

NORTHERN IRELAND
MUSEUMS
COUNCIL

Cover: Carved figure from White Island, gold bracelet from Cleenaghan and gold fastener from Tattykeel Lower

Published in 2003 by
Fermanagh District Council
Townhall, Enniskillen BT74 7BA

© Fermanagh District Council 2003
Helen Lanigan Wood has asserted her right under the Copyright, Designs and Patents Arc 1988 to be identified as the author of this work.

Designed by Carol Mc Gowan.
Printed by Carrick Print 2000 Ltd.
ISBN 0-9540727-1-5

www.enniskillencastle.co.uk

Contents

A Mesolithic family gets ready to roast a hare. The reconstruction of the hut in this model at Fermanagh County Museum is based on information from the excavation of a Mesolithic settlement at Mount Sandel, overlooking the river Bann, near Coleraine

t the end of the last ice age, the ice melted, sea levels rose and Ireland became an island separated from Britain. Later, in about 7000BC, people crossed the narrow stretch of water between Scotland and Ireland, in the period known as the Mesolithic or middle stone age. Soon afterwards they reached Fermanagh, travelling by log-boat along the rivers and lakes. The climate at the time was a few degrees warmer than today and thick pine forests covered most of the country, mixed with willow, juniper, hazel and birch.

People lived a nomadic lifestyle, fishing, hunting and gathering food. Fruit and vegetables grew wild in the countryside and there were many opportunities to hunt small game such as wild boar, fox, hare, wild cat and beaver and large animals such as the red deer. In Fermanagh, people settled for a while in the vicinity of Ross Lough and on the shores of Cushrush Island in Lower Lough Macnean, where some of the stone tools that they used have been found from time to time.

People used the natural materials around them to make tools, - animal bones, antler, wood and stone, but normally, in Fermanagh as elsewhere in Ireland, only their stone tools survive. They would have used animal skins as containers, for clothing and to provide shelter.

Clearing forests, building field walls and preparing the soil for planting are all part of a day's work for this Neolithic family.

he first farmers of Ireland came from Britain and mainland Europe around 4000BC bringing with them corn seeds and breeding animals. This period of time is called the Neolithic or new stone age because these early farmers still used stone tools such as axes, knives and scrapers. However, unlike their predecessors who had to hunt far and wide to survive, they were able to settle down on their farms and provide their own food. They lived in good-sized wooden houses, rectangular or circular in shape, and probably with thatched roofs. One of these rectangular houses was found at Ballynagilly, Co.Tyrone.

These early farming people believed in an afterlife and attached great importance to how they buried their dead. They built large stone burial chambers covered with mounds of earth and stone, which, unlike their timber houses, have survived in large numbers. In Fermanagh they are found mainly in the upland areas.

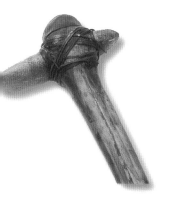

Neolithic Boat
A log-boat found in Lower Lough Erne at Rossfad has a Carbon 14 date of 3502-3350BC, so would have been used in the Neolithic period.

olithic people used this type of shed stone axe for cutting down s. It would have taken them less an hour to cut down a medium-d tree. One hundred and thirty e polished stone axes have n found in Fermanagh and one ese, from a bog at uiresbridge, had its apple-wood le still intact. The shaft in this ograph is modern.

Carbon 15 Dating
A radio carbon date is obtained by measuring the surviving radioactive carbon, Carbon 14, in wood, charcoal and other organic material. Since the carbon content of dead organic material decreases at a regular rate, these calculations can provide an approximate date, to within an average of two centuries.

The first farmers brought cattle, sheep and goats to Ireland as breeding stock and they would have used animal skins and hides for many purposes, including clothing. During excavations, archaeologists have frequently found bones from these animals and from the domesticated pig. These early farmers also brought barley and wheat seeds with them and remains of these tiny seeds have often been found during excavations.

This saddle quern found on the shore of Coolyermer Lough, was used for grinding corn. The corn was rubbed backwards and forwards with another stone until it was ground into flour. This type of quern was first used in the Neolithic and remained in use until the Iron Age when it was replaced by a more efficient hand mill called a rotary quern.

Neolithic people used arrows with flint points to hunt birds and small animals. For larger animals they used javelins, also with flint points. Arrows and javelins were also used in warfare.

There were three types of burial tombs in the Neolithic: Court Tombs, Portal Tombs and Passage Tombs. These and the later Wedge Tombs are called megalithic tombs, from the Greek words mega (great) and lithos (stone). All of these were communal burial places, a bit like family vaults, where the dead could be buried with the remains of their ancestors.

This Court Tomb at Aghanaglack had four large chambers for cremated burials and an open court area at either end which may have been used for funeral ceremonies. The cremated bones of two children were uncovered when this site was excavated in 1938 and everyday objects such as pottery containers and flint implements were also found. The mound of stone which once covered this grave is now gone.

Bronze working and pottery making in the Bronze Age. Bronze-smiths gradually developed their technical expertise and progressed from hammering out tools and weapons to casting them in two-piece stone moulds. Later, they added lead to bronze and used clay moulds to produce superbly crafted pieces.

The Bronze Age began about 2500BC when people discovered the new technology of metalworking. At first they produced copper tools and weapons, making the metal from copper ore mined in Ireland. Then they discovered that by importing tin and mixing it with copper, they could produce bronze, and that bronze tools and weapons were harder and more effective than copper ones. They also discovered gold in Ireland and made beautiful jewellery and decorative pieces. The Sperrin Mountains in Tyrone may have been the source for the gold objects found in Fermanagh.

New Burial Customs

Around 2300BC people began to bury their dead in individual graves and the old custom of communal burials in megalithic tombs gradually came to an end. These graves were either simple pits or lined with stone. They were often grouped together in a cemetery or in a mound, although they also occur as single graves. The bodies were often placed in a crouched position in the grave and, just as today, there was also the custom of cremating the body. Sometimes a small decorated pot (called a food vessel because its shape suggests that it could have been used to contain food or drink) was put in the grave. Later, cremated burials were protected by a large urn placed upside down over them. Towards the end of the Bronze Age it became the custom for cremated bones to be placed in an upright urn.

his vase-shaped food vessel and bronze dagger were found in a stone-lined grave inserted into a large stone mound on the summit of Topped Mountain. Also in the photograph is a strip of gold that once decorated the handle of the dagger. Gold rarely turns up in Bronze Age graves in Ireland and the person buried with this valuable dagger was obviously of some importance.

In the Bronze Age, Stone Circles, like this one from Drumskinny, may have been places for religious ceremonies, perhaps rituals involving sun worship. Signposts direct the public to Drumskinny Stone Circle, situated 4.5 miles N of Kesh.

Bronze Age Rock Art from the hillside above Boho at Reyfad, with an impressive design of concentric circles surrounding small round hollows. This type of art was usually carved on natural rock surfaces although one of the roof stones of a Wedge Tomb from Burren, near Blacklion Co Cavan, (H0790 3524) bears a similar design. Wedge Tombs, so called from the overall shape of the tomb, were first constructed in the late Neolithic and they continued to be built in the Early Bronze Age.

Bronze axe from Sraniff, near Derrygonnelly and bronze rapier sword found in Lough Erne. Both belong to the Early Bronze Age.

The technology of metal working spread throughout mainland Europe and was eventually brought to Ireland by people who used a distinctive type of pottery vessel called a beaker. These elegant pots were made all over Europe and one was found in Fermanagh, at Errasallagh, about five miles north-west of Roslea.

Copper was mined using a technique which involved lighting fires against the rockface. The heat fractured the rock and when cold water was poured suddenly over the heated surface, the rock shattered further. The miners then hammered out the copper ore, from which copper was made.

This Early Bronze Age gold lunula found in a bog at Cooltrain, north-east of Enniskillen, was made by beating out a rod of gold. Lunulas are never found in graves, perhaps because they were not personal ornaments but emblems of office worn by chiefs or priests and then passed on from one generation to the next.

This cast bronze spear was never properly finished. It was made towards the end of the Early Bronze Age and was found in the river Erne at Cloonatrig, near Lisbellaw.

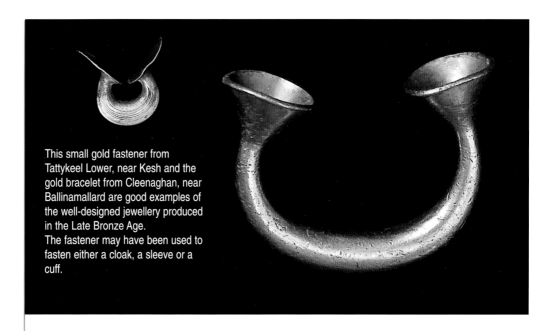

This small gold fastener from Tattykeel Lower, near Kesh and the gold bracelet from Cleenaghan, near Ballinamallard are good examples of the well-designed jewellery produced in the Late Bronze Age.
The fastener may have been used to fasten either a cloak, a sleeve or a cuff.

This cast bronze sword made in the Late Bronze Age was found in the Sillees River, near Ross Lough and was probably used in a slashing manner, perhaps by a warrior on horseback. The discovery of large numbers of Late Bronze Age spears, swords, rapiers and shields suggests that these were unsettled times with many people feeling the need to carry protective weapons.

These beads, made of imported amber, were found alongside the bronze knife and chisel in a bog in Killycreen West, near Belcoo. They were probably someone's prized possessions, buried for safe keeping in the Late Bronze Age and never retrieved.

Archaeological Excavations

Burial tombs excavated in Fermanagh include Court Tombs at Aghanaglack, Ballyreagh and Tully and Passage Tombs at Kiltierney and on Belmore Mountain. Sign-posts direct the public to Aghanaglack Court Tomb, situated 2.5 miles NE of Belcoo in Ballintempo forest.

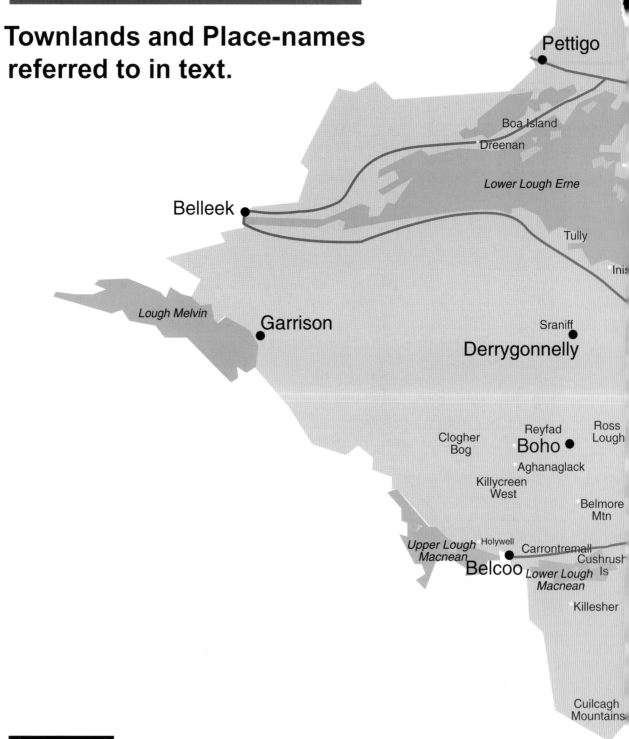

Map of Fermanagh

**Townlands and Place-names
referred to in text.**

Pettigo

Boa Island

Dreenan

Lower Lough Erne

Belleek

Tully

Inis

Lough Melvin

Garrison

Sraniff

Derrygonnelly

Reyfad

Ross
Lough

Clogher
Bog

Boho

Aghanaglack

Killycreen
West

Belmore
Mtn

Upper Lough
Macnean

Holywell

Carrontremall

Cushrush

Belcoo

Lower Lough
Macnean

Is

Killesher

Cuilcagh
Mountains

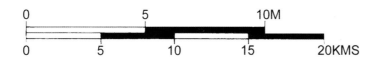

*Public Access

0   5   10M

0   5   10   15   20KMS

Ederney

Carn
Kiltierney
el

isnarick

Irvinestown

Ballinamallard

Rossfad
Cleenaghan

Coolcran

Cooltrain
Gortaloughan

Ballyreagh   Tempo

Fivemiletown

Devenish
Is

Topped
Mtn

Modeenagh

Portora
Enniskillen

Lough
Eyes

Drumee

Lisbellaw

Cleenish
Coolnashanton
Cloonatrig

Maguiresbridge

llanaleck

Errasallagh

Lisnaskea

Roslea

Upper Lough
Erne

Lisdoo

Kinawley

Benaughlin

Derrylin

Newtownbutler

Galloon

People discovered how to extract iron from iron ore sometime between 600 and 300BC and thus began the Iron Age when iron was first used to make tools and weapons. Small groups of Celtic warriors settled in Ireland around this time and may have been responsible for introducing the knowledge of iron as well as a new Celtic language and religion.

With the benefit of iron plough shares capable of ploughing heavy soils, Fermanagh people, previously confined to the light soils of upland areas, could now settle and farm in lowland areas. However, we know very little about either their homes or their burial places. At Kiltierney, near Ederney, they re-used a Neolithic Passage Tomb as a burial place, inserting a cremated burial in the mound of the Passage Tomb and all around it scattering cremated bones under little mounds.

No Iron Age pottery has been found in Ireland so we must assume that at that time people used wood or leather vessels in their homes. An unusual wooden cauldron from Fermanagh, found in Clogher Bog, is thought to be a copy of a metal Iron Age cauldron. These large metal cauldrons may have been used for communal feasts but they were also important in Celtic rituals and mythology. The most distinctive Iron Age artefact was the beehive rotary quern, a hand mill for grinding corn, and at least nine examples have been found in Fermanagh.

This is the upper stone of a decorated beehive quern found in Fermanagh. Called a rotary quern, the corn was poured through a hole in the upper stone and by the revolving motion of the upper stone on the lower one was ground easily into fine flour. This type of rotating hand mill was invented in the Iron Age and was a great improvement on the earlier saddle quern which required laborious rubbing to-and-fro

How to make iron

The blacksmith and his helpers dug iron ore out of the ground. This ore is quite plentiful in Ireland. Then they heated charcoal to a red-hot temperature in a furnace before adding the ore. They used a bellows to keep the temperature high and the heat smelted the ore, and separated the waste (the slag) from the actual iron.
The blacksmith then hammered the hot iron into shape, making excellent tools and weapons.

Celtic Religion

In the Iron Age people in Ireland spoke a Celtic language, the origin of present day Irish, and their religious beliefs appear to have had much in common with those of Celtic-speaking peoples in Britain and mainland Europe. They carved representations of their gods in stone, most frequently in the form of the human head, which was regarded as the seat of the soul and a symbol of divinity and supernatural power. They also erected impressive pillar stones decorated with distinctive Celtic designs of spirals and curving forms, the best example of which is at Turoe in county Galway. These carved idols and pillar stones must have been worshipped either at a ritual site such as the one discovered at Navan Fort in county Armagh or at some of the sacred Celtic places set in natural surroundings near springs, lakes, rivers, hilltops or trees.

Pagan festivals were celebrated at the beginning of the four seasons and in the middle of winter and summer. The harvest festival of Lunasa was held on the last Sunday of July or the first Sunday of August and was in honour of the god Lugh. The Irish name for August - Lúnasa - comes from this festival. The festivities included sports, dancing, singing and bilberry picking and because the festivals were later given a Christian meaning, many of the traditions associated with them survived until the 20th century. In Fermanagh these ancient festivals took place at the holy well of Dabhach Pádraig, at Holywell, near Belcoo and at six traditional hilltop sites, including Topped Mountain, Belmore Mountain and Benaughlin.

In Caldragh graveyard in the townland of Dreenan on Boa Island is an unusual stone carving consisting of two human figures set back to back, both with very large heads and crossed arms. Recently, the discovery in the graveyard of a missing fragment of the stone, revealed two elongated hands, one belonging to each figure. On the top of the stone, between the two heads, is a small hole like a socket. This powerful carving is usually considered to be pre-Christian and to provide evidence of the practice of Celtic religion in this part of Fermanagh. However, another view is that it was carved as late as the 9th or 10th century and had a Christian meaning.

According to the Celtic religion, the soul resided in the human head. Heads of kings and heroes were preserved and honoured. When enemies were killed, their heads were taken.

Celtic Warriors

The Celtic warrior groups who arrived in the Iron Age, probably came from France as well as from Scotland or northern England. These Celtic warriors were of high status and their exploits, including cattle raiding, horse racing, hunting, feasting and fighting, are described in Irish mythological tales. They fought with short iron swords, which they kept in beautifully decorated bronze scabbards. They also used long well-designed spears with iron tips and bronze butts. Their bronze horse harness equipment was particularly well made.

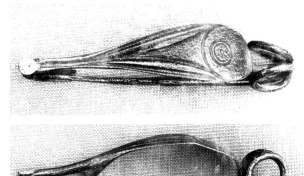

This bronze brooch designed like a modern safety pin was found in Modeenagh, near Tempo, and was used in the Iron Age, probably for fastening a cloak or shawl.

The Ogham alphabet had twenty letters and was based on the Latin alphabet of the late Roman Empire. In the case of inscriptions on stone, such as the example from Topped Mountain, the letters are formed by cutting groups of strokes across or on either side of the edge of the stone. The inscriptions begin at the bottom of the stone, climb towards the top and, if necessary, continue down the opposite side.

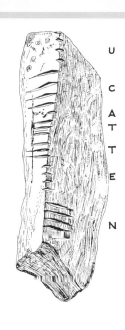

This stone probably commemorates a person called Nettacu, the name inscribed in Ogham writing along the edge of the stone. It was found at the edge of a prehistoric cairn on the summit of Topped Mountain. There are about 360 Ogham stones in Ireland dating from 300-700AD, with some commemorating pagan people and others bearing Christian inscriptions. They provide the earliest examples of written Irish and most of them are from the south-west of Ireland from the lands of the Desi people of Munster. They are also found in Wales, the Isle of Man and Scotland, in those areas colonized by the Irish at the end of the Roman period.

The Early Christian Period (500 - 1200AD)

The Early Christian or Early Medieval Period begins with the coming of Christianity and ends with the arrival of the Normans. During this time historical records began to be written down and so our knowledge of the period comes from history as well as from archaeology.

Although St. Patrick arrived in 432AD to convert Ireland to Christianity, the new religion replaced the old pagan beliefs very gradually. However, by the 6th century Christianity was established in Fermanagh and many monasteries were founded during that period. The main purpose of these early monasteries was religious with private prayer and penance being part of the daily routine. The monks attended at least six communal religious services – nocturns in the middle of the night, lauds at dawn, three services during the day and vespers in the evening. On Sundays and feast days they also attended Mass.

These monasteries were also places of learning and craftsmanship. Children from the upper classes were often fostered in the monasteries and educated in the monastic schools, monks devoted time to studying religious texts, and scribes and artists wrote and decorated gospel and psalm books made out of vellum. Many other objects were needed for use in the church, and specialist craftsmen worked in silver, bronze and gold to make beautiful chalices, bells, crosiers and shrines.

Each monastery was virtually self sufficient and produced all its own food. Most of the farm work was done by laymen who leased land from the monastery and probably lived outside the monastic enclosure with their wives and children. These children were entitled to free education in the monastic school. The monks kept cows, hens and bees and so were able of provide ample supplies of butter, cheese, eggs and honey. The main food was corn made up into loaves and gruel, and pork and beef were also eaten. A wide selection of fruit and vegetables was grown including onions, peas, beans, apples and strawberries. The monasteries also brewed their own beer and mead.

The Vikings raided St. Molaise's monastery on Devenish Island in 837AD

Monastic Buildings

There would have been numerous buildings within the monastic enclosure – small churches, monks' cells, refectories, granaries, workshops, scriptoria, even a guesthouse and a place to imprison local criminals. These were usually made of wood or other organic materials and have not survived. Later, stone was used and two of the oldest surviving stone buildings in Fermanagh were erected in the 12th century on Devenish Island– the small oratory called St. Molaise's Church and the Round Tower, one of the best preserved in the country.

One of the four carved heads decorating the cornice below the roof of the Round Tower on Devenish. Round Towers were first built in the 10th century as bell towers and they were also used for storing books, relics and other valuables. With doorways built above ground level, they served as places of refuge, particularly during attacks by Vikings.

Detail from a house-shaped shrine made in the 9th century AD and found with a similar shrine inside it in Lower Lough Erne, near Tully, midway between Belleek and Enniskillen. Made of yew with metal plates attached, these shrines would have held holy relics.

Vellum was made from calfskin. Craftsmen prepared the skin by soaking it in lime or excrement and then scraping off all the hair and fat. They tensioned the skin on a frame and rubbed it smooth with pumice stone. They usually used the skin of very young calves, although they preferred the stronger skin of a two to three-month old calf for elaborately decorated pages. To make a large gospel book like the Book of Kells, they could cut two double leaves from the older calf but only one from the younger. Using both sides of the page, each double leaf provided four pages. Around 185 calves were needed to make the Book of Kells.

Among the many early monasteries founded in Fermanagh are Galloon established by St. Tiernach, Inishmacsaint by St. Ninne, Killesher by St. Laiser, Cleenish by St. Sinnell, Kinawley by St. Naile and Devenish monastery, the most important of them, founded by St. Molaise.

The Early Christian Period (500 - 1200AD)

This bronze bell, which may have come from a monastery in Tyrone, was the type of hand-bell rung from the top windows of a Round Tower, to summon monks to prayer.

Front panel of the book-shrine, the 'Soiscel Molaise', made in the early 11th century to hold the gospel book of St. Molaise of Devenish. It shows the symbols of the four evangelists - the man for St. Matthew, the lion for St. Mark, the calf for St. Luke and the eagle for St. John – above and below the arms of a ringed cross. A plain bronze box inside this shrine was made in the 8th century.

One of the figures carved in the 9th or 10th century at a monastery on White Island in Lower Lough Erne; it holds a bell and crosier, symbols used for a bishop or an abbot. Six complete figures have survived on the site, each with a socket on top, suggesting that they served as supporting pillars. They seem to be designed in pairs, carved in three different heights. Used together, they could have supported the steps of an ambo, an early type of pulpit. Just as High Crosses of the period conveyed spiritual meanings through the depiction of biblical scenes, each of these figures communicated a Christian message. The Christian meaning is sometimes difficult to interpret today and, for a time, these figures were thought to be pre-Christian.

A High Cross once stood in Killesher graveyard and the head of this cross showing the figure of Christ crucified is now preserved in the Fermanagh County Museum. Fragments of High Crosses carved with biblical scenes still exist in Galloon and Boho graveyards and in Lisnaskea. A very fine plain High Cross can also be seen on the site of a monastery on Inishmacsaint island.

The Early Christian Period (500 - 1200AD)

Everyday Life in the Early Christian/Early Medieval Period

At this time most people lived and worked on farms. They enclosed their houses with a circular earthen bank and outer ditch, called a rath or ring-fort. In areas where stone was plentiful, they built the enclosure with dry-stone walling, and this is called a cashel. At first their houses were round; later they started to build square or rectangular houses, using stone in the cashels and various types of wood in the ring-forts, including timber frames, planks and post and wattle walls, daubed with clay. Some stone houses had dry-stone roofs but most houses were probably thatched.

More than 600 ring-forts are known in Fermanagh, and six of these have been excavated, at Boho, Coolcran, Drumee, Gortaloughan, Kiltierney and Lisdoo. Archaeologists also excavated a cashel at Carn where they uncovered an unusual souterrain (underground tunnel), made of earth and wood and dated by the tree-ring method (dendrochronology) to 820AD. Souterrains were usually made of stone and they were built in ring-forts and cashels to provide refuge against raiders and probably to store grain and dairy produce.

Life on a Crannog.
Some people preferred to live on an artificial island called a crannog. The name crannog, from the Irish word crann for tree, derives from the large amount of timber and brushwood used to build them. Stone, peat and soil were also used in their construction and all these materials formed a platform on which a house could be built.

With so many small lakes in Fermanagh, it is not surprising that 120 crannogs have been located in the county. The tree-ring dating method (dendrochronology) has provided dating for twenty-three of these. Only six belong to the Early Christian/Medieval Period, the rest date to the 14th century or later, a time when crannogs became popular again as defensive homesteads.

This bronze latchet found in the River Erne at Portora, Enniskillen, is an unusual type of brooch, probably used for fastening a woven cloak or shawl. Some latchets had loose bronze coils around their stem which made them very secure fasteners.

The Early Christian Period (500 - 1200AD)

Tree-ring dating or dendrochronology.

Growth rings on trees vary in width depending on the effect of wet and dry weather. These variations build up into an overall pattern stretching from today backwards in time. A date of around 570AD was obtained from a piece of oak from a crannog in Ross Lough in Fermanagh, by matching its tree-ring pattern with the overall pattern.

The larger pin is of gilded bronze and was part of a near complete ringed brooch, a bit like the brooch from Carrontremall (Illustrated below). The smaller pin made of bronze and decorated with enamel, is called a 'hand' pin because the top of it looks a bit like the fingers of a hand. Both pins were found in Fermanagh and belong to the Early Christian/Early Medieval period.

This horn, made between the 8th and 10th centuries AD, might have been played at a religious service, at an entertainment or perhaps, to lead an army into battle. Musicians playing similar horns are shown in scripture scenes on High Crosses. Made of yew with a copper mouthpiece and bronze mounts, it was found in the River Erne at Coolnashanton, south of Enniskillen.

This bronze brooch, decorated with enamel, was found in a quarry at Carrontremall, near Belcoo. This type of brooch was probably used to hold a cloak or shawl in place.

Further Reading

Many scholarly articles about the prehistory of Fermanagh can be found in the issues of the Ulster Journal of Archaeology, the Journal of the Royal Society of Antiquaries, and the Clogher Record.
Full references to these can be found in the bibliography contained in:
Williams, B. and Gormley, S. Archaeological Objects from County Fermanagh, Environment and Heritage Service, 2002.

Other publications containing information about Fermanagh's prehistory include :
DOE NI, Fermanagh: Its Special Landscapes, A Study of the Fermanagh Countryside and Its Heritage, 1991, Belfast (HMSO).
Hamlin, A. and Lynn, C. (eds) Pieces of the Past: Archaeological excavations by the Department of the Environment,
Belfast (HMSO), 1988.
Hickey, H., Images of Stone: Figure Sculpture of the Lough Erne Basin, 1985.
Neill, K (ed.) (forthcoming) An Archaeological Survey of County Fermanagh, DOE NI.
Rogers, M. Prospect of Erne: A Study of the Islands and Shores of Lough Erne, Co. Fermanagh, Belfast, 1967.
Rogers, M. Prospect of Fermanagh, Enniskillen, 1982.
Weir, A. Early Ireland: A Field Guide, Belfast, 1980.